Return to Earth

CHARACTERS

Narrator	Techno
Major Disaster	Breeze
Pine	Sunny
Willow	Terra
Dr. Cosmic	Foss
Optima	

SETTING

A space station,
far in the future

Narrator: Our story takes place three hundred years from now. We are a million miles from Earth on Space Station U-8410. This is where people went when Earth became too polluted. Earth's skies were dark with smog and truck emissions. Unable to breathe, people left Earth. Pine and Willow, teenage space cadets, grew up on Space Station U-8410. Major Disaster, commander of the space station, is explaining that their home now faces a problem.

Major Disaster: I have called you here because Space Station U-8410 is in a state of emergency. We have used up all but our last box of salt. And you know what that means.

Pine: Our pretzels will taste yucky!

Major Disaster: No! Without salt, we can't clean our air recycling system. Our space station will be doomed! We don't have trees here to make fresh air. We'll end up breathing dirty air.

Pine: That's what made our space station founders move here from Earth in the first place.

Major Disaster: Exactly. Your mission is to go back to Earth, polluted though it may be. You must return with as much salt as you can fit into the trunk of the Personal Space Transporter.

Willow: Where on Earth are we going to get salt?

Major Disaster: Dr. Cosmic will explain.

Narrator: Willow and Pine go to Dr. Cosmic's laboratory. He is the wisest person on the space station. He is also the weirdest person. Pine and Willow knock on Dr. Cosmic's door.

Willow: Knock, knock.

Dr. Cosmic: Who's there?

Willow and **Pine:** Willow and Pine.

Dr. Cosmic: Trees? On our space station? That is totally impossible. We can't grow trees here. Plus, trees can't talk. Although they can bark.

Narrator: Dr. Cosmic opens the door and lets in Pine and Willow.

Dr. Cosmic: Get it? Trees . . . bark.

Pine: You're a crack-up, Dr. C.

Willow: Major Disaster said you could get us ready for a special mission back to Earth.

Dr. Cosmic: Return to Earth? But nobody can breathe there! The air is polluted from centuries of burning coal and oil. It's just a brown, dead planet. What a shame, too. Earth used to be filled with beautiful trees. I wish we had real trees here. And wood. Then I could do my greatest experiment.

Pine: I'm afraid to ask, but . . . What is your greatest experiment?

Dr. Cosmic: I, Dr. Cosmic, will answer the question that has been on people's minds for ages: How much wood would a woodchuck chuck, if a woodchuck could chuck wood? You see, my mechanical woodchuck here is designed to chuck wood. If only we had trees . . .

Pine: Maybe one day. But first, we have to go back to Earth. We have to bring back salt so we can keep our own air clean.

Willow: Where on Earth are we going to get salt?

Dr. Cosmic: You can get it from the oceans, of course. They're filled with salt water. You'll have to use my Hydro-Sodio-Clorio Extracto machine. Also known as a salt sucker-outer.

Narrator: Dr. Cosmic gives Willow a little machine. It looks just like a juicer.

Dr. Cosmic: You pour in the salt water, then turn this crank. The water flows out the back, but the salt stays behind. You won't have much time to do the job, though, because the air on Earth is polluted. You must wear these gas masks.

Willow: We will!

Dr. Cosmic: Now, to get to Earth, take the Milky Way for two light years and turn left when you pass Mars.

Narrator: And so, Pine and Willow take off in their Personal Space Transporter. After a long journey, they see Earth in the distance. Dr. Cosmic was wrong! Earth isn't brown at all! It is blue and green swirls. Surprised, Pine and Willow put on their gas masks and fly in for a better look.

Pine: You know, you look pretty dorky with that gas mask on.

Willow: So do you. But at least we'll be able to breathe!

Pine: Hey, that's a person down there!

Willow: And she's not wearing a gas mask.

Pine: I'm taking the PST in for a landing in this field.

Narrator: Willow and Pine land in a field filled with flowers and buzzing bees. They climb out of their Personal Space Transporter. A friendly girl rides up on a bicycle.

Optima: Greetings and welcome to Earth! My name is Optima.

Willow: I'm Willow. This is Pine. We're from Space Station U-8410.

Pine: You're a human, just like us! And that's a bicycle. Wow! I've never seen a real one. Only a virtual one in a game.

Optima: This bike is solar-powered and has retractable wings. It can hop over rivers and cover long distances.

Pine: I'd like to try it sometime.

Willow: Optima, why aren't you wearing a gas mask? I thought the air on Earth was too polluted to breathe.

Optima: It was. But a few people thought there was hope for Earth. They stayed behind to clean up the planet even though they had to wear gas masks all the time. Those people were my ancestors.

Willow: It sure is nice here now. You and your ancestors have done an awesome job.

Optima: Thanks, but we're still not finished. Let me introduce you to some friends who are helping. By the way, you can take off those gas masks. The air is clean. And you do look a little . . .

Pine: Dorky?

Optima: You said it, not me!

Techno: Hello! My name is Techno. Nice Personal Transporter you have there!

Optima: Techno is a scientist. One really important thing Techno has done is find ways to stop spreading chlorofluorocarbons.

Pine: Clor . . . oh . . . what?

Techno: We call them CFCs for short. CFCs are certain types of gases that can harm the atmosphere. They nearly destroyed Earth's ozone layer. The ozone layer protects people from dangerous radiation.

Willow: So CFCs ruined Earth?

Techno: Well, they helped. CFCs break up when they are high in the atmosphere. They release a gas called chlorine. The chlorine destroys the ozone layer.

Optima: It was sunburn city!

Techno: Now we've stopped using CFCs. People can go outside again.

Optima: As long as they put on sunscreen.

Techno: Another big project of mine was using renewable resources to run cars and factories.

Optima: In the old days, nearly everything ran on fossil fuels, like oil and coal. They came from under the ground. It was getting harder to find them.

Techno: And even worse, oil and coal were used to run cars and factories. They were the main reason Earth's air was ruined. Now we have better ways to generate energy.

Willow: Whoa! My hat just blew off!

Breeze: Hi. I'm Breeze.

Optima: Breeze is wind power. See those wind generators over there?

Pine: Those tall things? I thought they were trees!

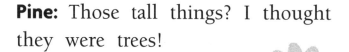

Optima: Nope. Trees are usually green and leafy. Those are wind generators. See the huge propellers? Breeze keeps the propellers spinning.

Breeze: I spin and Techno turns the spinning into electricity. Plus, I can blow forever!

Pine: Forever?

Breeze: Forever! That's why they call me a renewable resource. You know, there is nothing new about me. I've always been here on Earth.

Willow: Then what took you so long to help out?

Breeze: I offered to help people many times, but only a few paid attention.

Sunny: What about me?

Optima: Hi, Sunny. I was just about to introduce you. These visitors are from a space station.

Sunny: I'm solar power, another renewable resource. Shine, shine, shine every day, that's me. It's because of my happy face and sunny personality.

Breeze: Hmm. Are you trying to steal the spotlight again, Sunny?

Sunny: Well, I *am* the brightest thing around! No one can say that I'm not!

Techno: Solar panels catch and store Sunny's power. Then we turn the solar power into electricity and heat.

Breeze: We love helping, and we've always been there for people to use us.

Terra: Hi, all. I'm Terra.

Optima: Terra is a kid, just like you. She's our future. Sunny may be the brightest thing around. But Terra is the most important.

Pine: What do you do around here, Terra?

Terra: For starters, I help with recycling.

Willow: We do that at the space station, too.

Terra: I go on hikes into the woods to visit the frogs at my favorite pond. I watch the eagle's nest with my binoculars and let everyone know when the chicks hatch in spring.

Pine: I thought all the frogs and eagles on Earth had died because of the pollution.

Optima: Back when the air was polluted, frogs and eagles almost became extinct. But now that we have cleaned up Earth, they live anywhere they want. If the eagles can live happily, that means that the fish are also alive and well.

Terra: Whenever I go outside to explore, I keep my eyes and ears open for animals. When I see some, I take notes. Knowing that the animals are healthy helps Optima, Techno, and everybody else know that their cleanup is working!

Techno: Roger that! Terra's notes are a huge help.

Foss: Hi, everyone! What a great day!

Pine: Who's that?

Terra: Fossil Fuels. We call him Foss for short.

Willow: He's awfully happy!

Optima: He should be happy! He's retired.

Foss: And just in time. Everyone wanted a chunk of me. I nearly disappeared.

Willow: Sounds tough.

Foss: It was! What's worse, I got blamed for all kinds of nasty air pollution.

Terra: Foss tells me stories about how ugly Earth was in the old days. I'm glad we've cleaned up.

Foss: The trees and animals are so much happier now, too.

Pine: Trees? Animals? Hmm. Do you still have an animal called a woodchuck?

Foss: Sure. Woodchucks, groundhogs, everything is just like in the old days.

Willow: That is wonderful news.

Optima: Not everything is like it once was on Earth. We could use more people.

Terra: As long as they don't pollute!

Willow: Pine, are you thinking what I'm thinking?

Pine: I think I already thought what you're thinking!

Narrator: Pine talks into a transistor on his wrist.

15

Pine: Dr. Cosmic. This is Pine reporting from Earth. It's just as beautiful as you said it once was. Some brave people who stayed behind cleaned it up. The good news is: We can move back to Earth.

Willow: And even better news: They have real trees here.

Pine and **Willow:** And real woodchucks!

Narrator: Soon, Major Disaster and all the people at the space station returned to Earth. They joined Optima's team to restore the planet. Dr. Cosmic never did find out exactly how much wood a woodchuck could chuck. But everyone got solar-powered bicycles with retractable wings.

The End